All rights reserved. Published in the United States by Crown Books for Young Readers, an imprint of Random House Children's Books, a division of Penguin Random House LLC, New York.

Crown and the colophon are registered trademarks of Penguin Random House LLC.

Visit us on the Web! rhcbooks.com

Educators and librarians, for a variety of teaching tools, visit us at RHTeachersLibrarians.com

Library of Congress Cataloging-in-Publication Data is available upon request.

ISBN 978-0-553-53451-1 [trade]
ISBN 978-0-553-53452-8 [lib.bdg.]
ISBN 978-0-553-53453-5 [ebook]

10 9 8 7 6 5 4 3 2 1

MANUFACTURED IN CHINA   First Edition